GOOD GOSSIP
at the Backyard Table

GOOD GOSSIP
at the Backyard Table

SHIRLEY FRANCIS-SALLEY

Good Gossip at the Backyard Table

Copyright © 2024 Shirley Francis-Salley

Permission is granted to the buyer of this book to photocopy student material for use with Sunday school or Bible teaching classes.

All rights reserved. Except as noted above no part of this publication may be reproduced, stored in a retrieval system, or transmitted in any form or by any means - electronic, mechanical, digital, photocopy, recording, or any other - except for brief quotations and printed reviews, without written permission from

Clay Jars Publishing

Chester County, SC 29742

http://www.clayjarspublishing.com

Illustrations copyright © 2024 held by John McNees and NOW Illustration and Design

The author can be reached via email at:

contact@clayjarspublishing.com

Library of Congress Control Number: 2023907971

ISBN – 13: 978-0-9843369-8-2

Some of the Scripture texts in this work are taken from the following: NET Bible® copyright ©1996-2006 by Biblical Studies Press, L.L.C. http://netbible.com All rights reserved.

The names: THE NET BIBLE®, NEW ENGLISH TRANSLATION COPYRIGHT © 1996 BY BIBLICAL STUDIES PRESS, L.L.C. NET Bible® IS A REGISTERED TRADEMARK THE NET BIBLE® LOGO, SERVICE MARK COPYRIGHT © 1997 BY BIBLICAL STUDIES PRESS, L.L.C. ALL RIGHTS RESERVED. The ESV® Bible (The Holy Bible, English Standard Version®) copyright © 2001 by Crossway, a publishing ministry of Good News Publishers. ESV® Text Edition: 2011. The ESV® text has been reproduced in cooperation with and by permission of Good News Publishers. Unauthorized reproduction of this publication is prohibited. All rights reserved. *The Holy Bible: International Standard Version.* Release 2.0, Build 2015.02.09. Copyright © 1995-2014 by ISV Foundation. ALL RIGHTS RESERVED INTERNATIONALLY. Used by permission of Davidson Press, LLC.THE HOLY BIBLE, NEW INTERNATIONAL VERSION®, NIV® Copyright © 1973, 1978, 1984, 2011 by Biblica, Inc.® Used by permission. All rights reserved worldwide. God's Word Translation Scripture is taken from GOD'S WORD®, © 1995 God's Word to the Nations. Used by permission of Baker Publishing God's Word Translation Group. Scripture quotations marked (NLT) are taken from the Holy Bible, New Living Translation, copyright © 1996, 2004, 2007 by Tyndale House Foundation. Used by permission of Tyndale House Publishers, Inc., Carol Stream, Illinois 60188. All rights reserved. Scripture taken from the New King James Version®. Copyright © 1982 by Thomas Nelson. Used by permission. All rights reserved.

~ Dedication ~

To God, my Heavenly Father, God the Son, God the Holy Spirit; One God eternal.

He has given me the gift of imagination and a love of sharing it through the written word. By His Holy Spirit He has filled me with the desire to use this precious gift for His good purpose.

I am a Writer.

In His Service.

CONTENTS

PREFACE 1

INTRODUCTION 5

PART I: DID YOU HEAR ABOUT…? 9
    PRICELESS {ACT ONE} 11
    RECOGNIZED! 17
    IT'S TIME 25
    DRENCHED 31

PART II: HERE'S WHAT I WAS TOLD 35
    GHOSTED 37
    A TALE OF TWO WORLDS… 43
    TIME 49
    IFS, BUTS AND THENS 57

PART III: SPICY INFORMATION! 65
    MY BOAZ IS MARRIED 67
    THE LUGGAGE UNDER HIS BED 75
    WAITING 81
    CLUTCHED PEARLS 89

PART IV: CAN'T KEEP THIS TO MYSELF 95
    TOUCH IT, FEEL IT, TASTE IT 97
    SENT ONE…WENT ONE 101
    FAMILY PERKS 107
    THE TERRIBLE T'S 113

PART V: RUMOR HAS IT! 119
    JUNK FOOD 121
    PRICELESS {ACT TWO} 129

EPILOGUE 133

ACKNOWLEDGEMENTS 135

MEET THE AUTHOR 137

PREFACE

When people hear the word "Gossip", some will head for the nearest exit. Some will eagerly lick their lips as they wait for hopefully scintillating or scandalous news about someone else. And then there are those who want to use the information they obtain to share with others because it gives them a sense of power and being in the know.

Gossip is **shared information** that is almost always thought of as a negative practice, usually preceded by such phrases as:

"I should keep this to myself, but I can't…"

"Pssst! Did you hear about…?"

"You didn't hear this from me, but let me tell you…"

"I overheard…"

"Got any spicy information for me?"

Some might say gossip should never be thought of as anything good or useful. They'd say sharing words or enlightening another about the actions and goings on of someone else's life serves no good purpose and should not be repeated even if it's rumored to be true. But we are living in an information society full of people who want or need to be informed. As long as there is "news" to be shared there will always be gossipers and gossipees. That being said, the source of the information given must always be considered.

I've often wondered, can anything good be said of gossip when just the thought of the word can conjure up an image of two people in an empty breakroom with their heads together spilling tea about another coworker?

Let's face it. We've all been talked about or gossiped about at some time in our lives. And I admit I've done my share of gossiping, too. It hurts when someone passes on a story that was meant for their ears only, and even more when they misinterpret or misconstrue what was shared with them in confidence.

If ever there was such a thing as a *Hearer's Guide on When to Receive Gossip as "Gospel"* it should include tips.

- Look at the relationship the gossiper has with the one who is the subject of the gossip.

- Measure the importance, influence, and popularity of the one who is the subject of the gossip.

This kind of critical thinking will help determine how much is to be believed and accepted by the hearer.

The late Alan Redpath, well-known British pastor, evangelist and author once advised that any gossip we are privy to should be run through the THINK test before we consider the thought of sharing or ingesting the *"juicy* morsel" about to be served. This applies whether you are the gossiper or the gossipee*.

Redpath says: THINK:

- **T** – Is it true?
- **H** – Is it helpful?
- **I** – Is it inspiring?
- **N** – Is it necessary?
- **K** – Is it kind?

Now, it has been said by some that gossip *can* be good.

My book's message devotes itself to the idea that gossip, good or bad, falls under the category of shared information and news. As I take on the role of the gossiper, and share these fictitious stories that are, in a sense, real because they imitate life, let me say, the trials and certainly the temptations we face are not uncommon. For some, a ring of familiarity might be found among these pages.

From cover to cover, my aim is to transform the negative thoughts and practices that surround the sharing of *common gossip* into the sharing of *good gossip*. To partake in offering information or news about things that are excellent and praiseworthy; admirable and noble; right and pure. These kinds of thoughts and practices can surely pass the THINK test. They are the perfect antidote for quenching fiery darts.

--Shirley Francis-Salley

---

* note Wisdom to Live By, Christian Focus Publications, 1998, p. 41. Used by Permission

INTRODUCTION

Does Gossip Have a Seat at the Table?

Today, no home is complete without its table. It may be found in the kitchen, the dining room, the living room, the patio, or in the backyard. It's where we come to sit down beside one another, and the weight of standing is alleviated. Tired feet are refreshed, and bread is broken. Hungry appetites are satisfied, thirsts are quenched, and itching ears are scratched and soothed with the latest "news" and common gossip.

But there is so much more to experience at the table. There is the offering up of community and intimacy, a space for the parts that we keep quiet on the inside to be said out loud. At the table feelings are shared. Ideas are candidly exchanged. Hearts are laid bare. Tears are shed. Tears are dried. Relationships and hopes are renewed.

Whether your table is located in the kitchen, the dining room, the living room, the patio, or in the backyard, this book invites you to come and eat Spirit-healthy portions of the rich Bread of Life and its oh so sweet inspiration. What a blessing it truly can be when you're in the company of family, friends, and even new connections while words such as, "This is too good;

I can't keep it to myself!" or "I've just got to tell somebody!" are going around the table.

When you start telling what you've heard and what you know about the goodness of God, that's when "Good Gossip" will be flowing.

If the table happens to be in the backyard it adds another level to the blessing because it will be happening in the surroundings of God's beautiful green trees and grass and under His blue or starry skies.

And so, with that in mind, an invitation to a seat at this backyard table is being extended to you.

I heard it through the Grapevine that Jesus said, without Him we can do nothing.

John 15:1, 5 NLT

1 *"I am the true grapevine, and my Father is the gardener."*

5 *"Yes, I am the vine; you are the branches. Those who remain in me, and I in them, will produce much fruit. For apart from me you can do nothing."*

Romans 10:17 NLT

"So faith comes from hearing, that is, hearing the Good News about Christ".

PART I

Did You Hear About...?

Whoever is generous to the poor lends to the Lord, and he will repay him for his deed.

Proverbs 19:17 ESV

PRICELESS {ACT ONE}

On the drive over, the woman closed her eyes and thought back to all the months of what she felt had been a lot of pushing and prodding to get her to the space she was in at this moment. She thought about the conversations, and invitations she'd always politely refused.

But on a particular day her usual responses of "I don't know", and "Well, maybe, we'll see…" became a solid "Yes, okay, I'll go."

However, there were strings attached to her yes. She recalled the particular conversation where she'd finally made a confession to her persistent line partner at the conveyer plant where she worked:

"I don't have any clothes to wear. Haven't you noticed I've been wearing the same pair of leggings and two blouses for the last 3 weeks? I'm surprised nobody else is saying something about it. The way people talk. Somebody in the shelter where I'm staying stole my clothes. All I have left are the clothes on my back, and a blouse that was under my pillow."

She remembered her line partner saying: "It's bad when you need shelter within the shelter. You should have said something to me."

The woman would never forget how she felt that next day when her line partner handed her a large bag.

"Here, I got something for you."

She opened the store bag and pulled out a skirt, a sweater, a blouse, and a pair of shoes. As surprised and as instantly grateful as she was, her first words were, "How much did you pay for these things?" Then she noticed the sales receipt.

"A hundred and fifty dollars? That's way too much to spend on me. I can't afford to pay you back. It's too pricey!"

Her friend replied, "There's no excuse now. You're coming to church with me Sunday. I'm sure God has a message with your name on it!"

"My name?

"Yes, your name. And you will **NOT** be paying me back. It's my gift to you. Besides, you could never have enough to pay me back because, God is giving me the privilege and opportunity of watching you enter His house, that's priceless!"

With a sighed hesitancy the woman answered, "Okay, I'll come!"

The Way I See It…

As Christians, we know that God IS good, and He is always working for good outcomes in our life situations. There are those who do not realize this truth. Some feel they don't need God. Still others feel they're not worthy. And then there are those who feel they are too insignificant to even matter. They travel the road of life never experiencing the abundant life and love Christ came to give. Never understanding the GIFT that is ours to take hold of. Those who know and realize, are uniquely equipped and purposely positioned in the lives of those who don't know. God blesses people through people. Sharing our faith is a blessing to God, to others, and to ourselves.

GOOD GOSSIP!

Mark 16:15-16 NLT

And then he told them, "Go into all the world and preach the Good News to everyone. Anyone who believes and is baptized will be saved. But anyone who refuses to believe will be condemned."

Psalm 96:2-3 NLT

Each day proclaim the good news that he saves. Publish his glorious deeds among the nations. Tell everyone about the amazing things he does.

Let's Pray

We will bless You, O Lord, at all times. Father, You give us a reason to praise Your name every moment, every hour, every day. You've been so good to us, and You continue to keep us in your care. We praise You with our whole hearts and we bless and give You glory just because of who You are. Lord, let the fruit of Your Spirit rise up in us and work through us to give hope, comfort and friendship as we reach out to share our faith and testimonies with those You place on our path.

Lord God, please continue to bless us. Provide for us as only You can so that at all times we will have everything we need, to abound in every good work our hands find to do. In Jesus' name we ask. Amen.

Behold, I stand at the door and knock. If anyone hears my voice and opens the door, I will come in to him and eat with him, and he with me.

Revelations 3:20 ESV

RECOGNIZED!

The taste of the warm sausage biscuit and the coffee just the way she liked it soothed her morning hunger. Suddenly, she heard a voice.

"Hey, I know you! Weren't you on that talent show?"

The woman looked up from her Bible into the face of a teenaged girl.

"You were on *The Voice!* I watched you with my mom! Can I sit here?"

Before the older woman could answer, the young girl plopped down, almost overturning the pineapple smoothie she was balancing on her tray.

"I love how you all had to sing to those music coaches on *The Voice*, while they had their backs turned to you. All they heard were your voices."

The woman smiled ever so slightly and gazed off into a moment of reminiscence. She responded wistfully, "Yes I remember."

She lingered in that moment of days gone by, and heard herself softly say, "Those **coaches heard my voice and were moved so much they all turned around.**"

RECOGNIZED!

The young girl leaned in, attempting to hear the woman more clearly. Her clumsy, sudden movement brought the woman's attention back to the present moment.

She added, "I was so happy to be chosen, to be a part of something that was so great and awesome. It was the beginning of a wonderful relationship with *The Voice*. And the hopes of becoming a winner. I'll never forget how that moment felt. But that was almost ten years ago, young lady."

"I know," replied the young girl. I was about eight years old back then. We always watched *The Voice*. I've always wanted to be a singer, performing in the bright lights with people hearing my voice and loving it. There was a rumor going around back then that you got robbed by the producers. People were saying YOU should have been the winner."

The woman grinned broadly at this and said, "Oh, but I did win!"

"How's that?" Asked the young girl, with a look of puzzlement in her eyes.

The woman placed her book marker in her Bible and closed it.

She looked intently at the young girl and said, "I don't know what you know about the Lord but let me share something with you."

The girl leaned in eager to know what the woman meant about being a winner.

The woman continued speaking, "**Remembering** *The Voice* always takes me back to how I was living my life back then. I walked with my back to God's truth, and I walked in a truth of my own. But one day, sight unseen, I heard a voice that was so soft and yet so powerful. It moved me. And like those coaches, I just had to turn around to see who it was.

That was the day I faced the TRUTH.

That was the day I made a choice.

That was the day a relationship started.

That was the day I became a winner.

That was the day I heard the VOICE."

RECOGNIZED!

The Way I See It...

Have you ever wanted to be chosen for something you knew you were great at? Something that would put your name in lights and give you star power? But you weren't picked. Your name wasn't called while competing in life's contests. If you've been in that position, then you know how it feels.

Sometimes things don't seem fair. We don't get the things and accolades we feel we should have gotten. We find ourselves reminiscing on what could have been if only we'd won and gotten our 15 minutes of fame. But when you compare 15 minutes of fame to an eternity of life in Christ, is there really any comparison or contest?

You might not be chosen, or hear your name called, by the world but when you are chosen by God, and hear your name called by the Good Shepherd, and answer the call, to come into His sheepfold, you are a WINNER indeed. It is in Christ Jesus that we have victory. In Christ Jesus, we WIN!

Have you heard the VOICE this day?

GOOD GOSSIP!

John 10:26-27 NKJV
My sheep hear My voice, and I know them, and they follow Me. And I give them eternal life, and they shall never perish; neither shall anyone snatch them out of My hand.

Hebrews 3:7-8 NKJV
"Today, if you will hear His voice Do not harden your hearts..."

1 Corinthians 15:57
But thanks be to God, who gives us the victory through our Lord Jesus Christ.

Let's Pray

O Blessed Savior, help us to hear above all, Your Voice, as You call to those who know You for the pardoning of their sins. And for those who are yet to know you, yet to hear Your Voice. Let the sound of Your Voice be a sweet and irresistible sound that causes them to turn to you and respond with the words, "I yield, I yield. What must I do to be saved?"

We pray, In Jesus' name. Amen.

For this my son was dead, and is alive again; he was lost, and is found. And they began to be merry.

Luke 15:24 KJV

It's Time…

Mamie: Heyyy, ain't seen you in quite some time!

Ernestine: Well, I'll be! Mamie! Yess, it's been a while.

Mamie: What you doin' on the bus this mornin'?

Ernestine: Car actin' up. Had to take the bus yesterday too, just so I can get to work. But it's in the shop now. I'll have it back tomorrow!

Mamie: So, how you been, you still live on Wilson street? How's Roberta?

Earnestine: Oh nooo, I left there three years ago and me and Roberta ain't friends no more. We stopped speaking 'bout 4 years ago.

Mamie: I thought I heard something 'bout that, but, you know…My goodness! Y'all was tighter than 2 peas in a pod.

Ernestine: Yeah I know… saw her on the bus yesterday. She got on with some man that I don't know. They sat down in the seat right in front of me. She didn't notice me 'cause I held my magazine up to my face. I could hear their conversation, though. She called him Jackson. He was talking to her about his son. Here's what I heard…

IT'S TIME...

Jackson: He's my son and he'll always be my son. Nothing can ever change that, but we have not spoken to each other in twelve years.

Roberta: Twelve years! Man, that's a long time.

Jackson: Yesterday out of the clear blue sky, I get a call from him. He wants to see me. He wants to repair our broken relationship. He wants to come home.

Roberta: How do you feel about that?

Jackson: Well, nothing could ever separate us from the biological fact of him being my child. We got the same blood. But his way of living caused an awful break in our relationship, and we had to part ways. He moved out in anger and wouldn't return my calls. So finally, I just stopped calling.

Roberta: Man, that's gotta hurt! So, for twelve years he's been missing out on all the great things I heard you been doing for your other children?

Jackson: Yep!

Roberta: Well, it serves him right! He doesn't deserve any of those things that you're doing for your other children. Did you hang up on him?

Jackson: Nope.

Roberta: So, what did you say to him?

Jackson: I'll leave the door unlocked and the porch light on...

The Way I See It...

Is this you? Are you like Jackson's son? You know you're a child of God but your relationship with God, your Father, is propped up on its last leg; broken, or maybe even dead? Not because of God, but because of you.

Nothing and no one but you, can separate you from the love, blessings, and undeserved favor God has for you, His child. He is a Good, Loving, and Forgiving, Heavenly Father. Come on home, child of God; it's time!

GOOD GOSSIP!

Ephesians 1:7-8 NLT

He is so rich in kindness and grace that he purchased our freedom with the blood of his Son and forgave our sins. He has showered his kindness on us, along with all wisdom and understanding.

Romans 8:38-39 NLT

And I am convinced that nothing can ever separate us from God's love. Neither death nor life, neither angels nor demons, neither our fears for today nor our worries about tomorrow—not even the powers of hell can separate us from God's love. No power in the sky above or in the earth below—indeed, nothing in all creation will ever be able to separate us from the love of God that is revealed in Christ Jesus our Lord.

James 4:8 NLT

Come close to God, and God will come close to you.

Let's Pray

O Father God, some of Your children have wandered off from the Love, Light and Life that is You, O Lord. There is nothing that is too hard or impossible for You. Speak to their spirits, open the eyes and ears of their understanding. Turn their hearts towards you. Awake in each of them a burning desire to seek You and come back to their home in Your Kingdom where You reign in love, truth, and righteousness forever.

In Jesus' name, amen.

The LORD is my shepherd; I shall not want.

Psalms 23:1 NKJV

Drenched

―――✦―――

She pressed against the storefront buildings that stood alongside each other while trying to shield herself with the little bits of cover they provided. The friendly skies of moments earlier were friendly no more. They opened up and began to pour out what seemed like tub loads of rain.

"I could kick myself," she whispered inwardly. She hadn't paid attention to the morning weather report. So, she did not hear the meteorologist's words "Expect heavy rain this morning."

Without an umbrella, making a run for it was out of the question. Getting her hair wet spelled disaster and she couldn't afford to ruin the silk blouse she'd bought the day before. Her intentions were to return it right after the job interview she was trying to get to. She had no other choice but to wait for the downpour to stop. She looked at her watch knowing she was going to be late to the interview for this job she desperately needed. She was in a pickle of a fix.

"Lord, You know they're saying I was laid off so the boss' sister could have my job. Lord, You know that wasn't right or fair. You know I need this new job. They're probably having a water cooler conversation about me this very minute!"

No sooner had she said that something came into her view. It was a passerby sheltered under a large umbrella with two words on it: JESUS SAVES. And in her heart she heard, "I am all you need. My grace is sufficient for you."

In that moment two things happened. The heavy rain simmered down to a light, but steady shower, and she made a decision.

She said to herself: "I'm going! I won't be able to return this blouse once it's wet, and my hair is going to be a mess. I might even be turned away, but I am going to this interview. In Jesus name."

She stepped out from the building's cover, into the showers, head tilted back, mouth wide open, arms outstretched, not caring about hair, or clothing, or rejection. She raised the volume of her voice and said, "Hallelujah Anyhow! Drench me, Lord. I know you've got me! Soak me with your showers of blessings that are on the way for me!"

The Way I See It...

We are God's most precious creation, and that which God creates He remains responsible for. Thank You, Jesus!

♪ *"His eye is on the Sparrow, and I know He watches me."* ♪

GOOD GOSSIP!

He is Dependable:

Isaiah 41:13 NLT

For I hold you by your hand-- I, the Lord your God. And I say to you, don't be afraid I am here to help you.

He Keeps His Promises:

Numbers 23:19 NLT

God is not a man, so he does not lie. He is not human, so he does not change his mind. Has he ever spoken and failed to act? Has he ever promised and not carried it through?

He Honors His Commitment to Us:

Romans 8:32 NLT, 2 Corinthians 9:8 NIRV
Since he did not spare even his own Son, but gave him up for us all, won't he also give us everything else?

2 Corinthians 9:8 NIRV
And God is able to shower all kinds of blessings on you. So in all things and at all times you will have everything you need.

Let's Pray

O Father God, thank You for being our shelter; our hiding place, and for being our trustworthy parent in whom we keep our faith. Lord Jesus, in the midst of it all and through it all, let this mindset be in us; that whatever comes our way, You are our Protector who goes before us and defends us from behind. We put our trust in You, O Lord. In Your Mighty name we pray. Amen.

PART II

Here's What I Was Told

Let all that I am praise the LORD; may I never forget the good things he does for me. He forgives all my sins and heals all my diseases. He redeems me from death and crowns me with love and tender mercies. He fills my life with good things. My youth is renewed like the eagle's!

Psalms 103:2-5 NLT

GHOSTED

Their eyes stumbled upon each other and locked in place. They were in the same space but there was a divide that had been created by the neatly arranged chairs in the vast meeting room.

She felt the pull of his magnetic energy as he made his way across the room towards her, never once breaking eye contact. In that instant she knew he had felt it, too. They exchanged subdued verbal pleasantries of introduction, but it was the warm handshake they shared that had her aroused and bubbling over on the inside. A spiritual connection had been made and she was so glad about it. The meeting they were attending was now over, but their usual and established activities and assignments called them to different directions, and they went their separate ways.

Within less than an hour of her arriving home she received a text message. It was from him. He'd found her on social media and reached out. From that day on they were in contact every day. They talked about everything and anything. She loved how he shared his dreams and visions with her, taught her things she did not know, and she did the same to him. She had found a friend. Their connection was so familiar, and comfortable. It was easy and she knew it would go on forever. Or so she thought…

They'd shared very few in-person encounters in the nearly three months since they'd met. Their three months of time spent together was in the constant back-and-forth texting to each other without invitation or formality as they shared, laughed, and bonded with each other like giddy teenagers. And suddenly without indication or warning he disappeared. For two weeks she kept reaching out to him hoping for an explanation but there was no reply.

It was as if he had dropped off the face of the Earth. She felt the sting of rejection and betrayal. It saddened her to the point of tears for many days and she never heard from or saw him again. His less than caring act of ghosting displayed his lack of courage, and integrity. It crippled her. But in the passing of time, she gave up the ghost and when she thought of him, the hurt was no more. She had come to understand and realize the beauty of her self-worth and identity. And that meant more to her than any digital relationship. It was his loss, not hers.

The Way I See It...

What happens when someone is ghosted? A relationship is brought to a jolting stop. Communication is broken. The one being ghosted, the ghostee, is not given a say in the matter. Have you ever been ghosted? There is no closure. Being ghosted can make one feel confused; undesired; unappreciated; unworthy; disrespected and alone.

But what does that say about the character of the ghoster? The one doing the ghosting. It is possible that person might be on "empty" when it comes to compassion, or courage, or maybe even maturity. And if the ghoster is lacking in all of these areas, the ghostee should consider themself very fortunate to have gotten ejected from the "toxic relationship" bus. Who needs that?!

But here's a thought...is the same sort of thing going on when arguably for some, but inarguably for others the most **precious relationship** we could ever have has lost its value and doesn't matter like it used to? Too busy with life to share intimate moments of time that can't be retrieved? Are feelings of anger, hurt or guilt impeding the relationship? Is a complete unfriending or blocking the next step? Are we, ...are you, ghosting Jesus? To do so is a dangerous thing and can only lead to Spiritual death.

GOOD GOSSIP!

Deuteronomy 6:5 NLT

And you must love the LORD your God with all your heart, all your soul, and all your strength.

James 4:8 NLT

Come close to God, and God will come close to you.

John 15:4-5 NLT

Remain in me, and I will remain in you. For a branch cannot produce fruit if it is severed from the vine, and you cannot be fruitful unless you remain in me. "Yes, I am the vine; you are the branches. Those who remain in me, and I in them, will produce much fruit. For apart from me you can do nothing."

Let's Pray

O Precious Lord, You are our Heavenly Father and our God. We thank You just for who You are. You are Lord of all, and we worship You. It is our desire to use this space in time to share our hearts with you. Increase our awareness of Your presence in our lives. Let us not neglect the daily seeking of Your counsel. Increase our understanding of Your love for us and Your desire to walk and talk with us. In times of decision strengthen us to say, "Yes" to Your will and way and, "No" to ours. We are nothing without You, Lord. Without You we are lost and alone. Hear our prayer, O God, and lead us in the way of light and understanding. In Jesus' name we pray. Amen.

For God did not send His Son into the world to condemn the world, but that the world through Him might be saved.

John 3:17 NKJV

A Tale of Two Worlds...

She was a child of the night; born into a world and in a space in time that she did not choose. They all said she was one of those "Bad Girl" types that Donna Summer sings about. Growing up hard. Robbing and stealing, they said. And giving herself away for money and power were the sinful deeds she used to keep herself afloat.

After a time, the long arms and wide hands of the law snatched her up and would not let her go. Brought before an outraged accuser, twelve angry jurors, and a book-throwing judge, she was condemned and sent to prison for her crimes.

And when, and if, it was lawfully determined that she had sufficiently paid for her crimes and had been rehabilitated enough to go and sin no more, then and only then, would she be set free. No one cared about her back story and how the events of her life had brought her to this place. No one cared but Jesus.

And though still imprisoned and serving not just her time, but serving the worldly choices she'd made, she was set free in her soul, her mind, and her spirit because she came to know Jesus and received his unparalleled pardon that released her from her guilt and sin.

But there was another woman born into the same world, in another time of existence, an ancient time. It, too, was a world she did not choose. She, also, was guilty and condemned by her accusers to a sentence of death by stoning which was the accustomed penalty for deeds such as hers.

On her day of reckoning in that ancient world, a willful crowd of self-appointed judges, made up of scribes and Pharisees, brought her before the One whom they called Teacher. They expressed their lawful right to exact from her their pound of flesh in payment for her sinful deeds.

But the woman was more so being used by the accusing crowd of religious leaders as a stumbling block to disadvantage this Teacher whom, though teaching among them, was not of their world.

He inhabited a Kingdom that was totally different from this world in which the woman was struggling to survive. He was a Teacher and He was also a "Righteous Judge". His name? Jesus. And as she stood before him, she called him Lord.

The Way I See It...

And from His Kingdom, He gave both women the gifts of "mercy and no condemnation".

And He did this BEFORE He freed them from the hands of certain death and enfolded them in arms of Eternal Life.

Be it modern world or ancient world, sin, no matter what kind, or to what degree, is still sin. And Jesus, thanks be to God, is still Jesus.

Like the women of both worlds, while we were yet in our sins, Jesus the Christ made the greatest exchange of all time. He took our sins and our unescapable sentences of death, upon Himself and in return He gave us freedom; and the newness of born-again life that is eternal in Him. Hallelujah!

The love of Jesus has no expiration date. He shows and offers his love to the unnamed and unsaved women of this modern world just as he did to the unnamed and unsaved adulterous woman in the Bible's Book of John. It's up to us to embrace His love.

GOOD GOSSIP!

Romans 8:1-2 NLT

So now there is no condemnation for those who belong to Christ Jesus. And because you belong to him, the power of the life-giving Spirit has freed you from the power of sin that leads to death.

John 8: 7, 9-11 NLT

7 They kept demanding an answer, so he stood up again and said, "All right, but let the one who has never sinned throw the first stone!"

9 When the accusers heard this, they slipped away one by one, beginning with the oldest, until only Jesus was left in the middle of the crowd with the woman.

10 Then Jesus stood up again and said to the woman, "Where are your accusers? Didn't even one of them condemn you?"

11 "No, Lord," she said.

And Jesus said, "Neither do I. Go and sin no more."

Let's Pray

Dear Lord Jesus, if it weren't for Your love, where would we be? Thank You, Lord, that we are not condemned. We are no longer bound by sin. We cherish Your gift of Salvation. And those You have set free by Your work on that old, rugged cross are free indeed. In Your great and holy name, we pray. Amen and amen.

LORD, remind me how brief my time on earth will be. Remind me that my days are numbered— how fleeting my life is.

Psalms 39:4

TIME

~~~~~~~~~~~~~~

Time sat in the driver's seat doing 80 miles an hour. He never did anything less. The woman had handed him the keys. And even though it was her ride, and her life, Time watched her climb into the backseat just as she'd been doing since the day she'd come of legal age to possess a driver's license.

Time had always had the freedom to navigate every journey she'd ever planned or taken. He could not recall a time she'd ever acted wise enough, been brave enough, or even curious enough to take the wheel from him and chart her own course to success and time of arrival. He knew she'd always be content to just sit back and let him take care of everything. After all, Time was her friend and he had been good to her, until now.

By now… Time had seen enough of her life, and heard enough of it. He'd been patient with all of her starts and stops. He had fixed a lot of things, and let a lot of things go, hoping she would realize his true value. But now, he was tired. He would wait no more.

He controlled the steering wheel with one hand and used the other hand **to puff on the cigarette he held tightly between his lips.** It was filled with the memories of all her dead dreams, faded visions, and moments of "what could have been".

TIME

He purposely flicked its hot ashes out of his opened window, knowing the wind would blow the glowing, memory-filled embers into the open rear window she sat at. From the rear-view mirror, Time watched the hot embers graze the soft skin of her cheek. He knew she felt the painful burn of her undying memories, unfulfilled dreams, and faded visions.

They say, "All good things must come to an end." Time embodied that saying to its fullest as he let go of the steering wheel that sent the woman careening down a deep embankment and crashing headlong into the place called End. The news of her misfortune was quickly spread.

Time had been in her life to be a help and a resource to her, but he was not valued or appreciated. Instead, the woman had given herself and all her attention to another and this other had persistently enchanted and engaged her with irresistible distractions. Yet here at the place called End, he had not even come to mourn her passing. His name? Procrastination.

The Way I See It...

Navigating through the business of everyday living and accomplishment can be very flustering because there are so many things in your life that are pulling at you and vying for your time and attention.

However, your dreams, visions, and goals are vital and valuable to you also. So, you devised a plan, a schedule to keep you on track.

You cut down or cut out those time-consuming activities that just don't support your Heaven-sent dreams and visions.

You understand that "Discipline is the bridge between goals and achievement." You've memorized that Jim Rohn quote.

You're spending less time on the phone and social media; watching less television, and you're hitting the sack an hour later or rising an hour earlier just to achieve the goals you've set.

You don't allow yourself to be distracted because you know that when you open the door to Distraction it most likely won't be alone. It will be accompanied by its best friend, Procrastination. Those two are the enemies of Time. And they have only come to rob you of your blessings.

TIME

Time is a terrible thing to waste. Make the most of what you have been given. Value your time. It is a precious gift and resource. But even more so, value your time with God for He is the Giver of this precious gift, and He values you.

It is most beneficial to set aside a daily time just for you and God. Guard that time! Grow your relationship with Him through a discipline of spiritual practices such as worshiping, praying, reading, studying, fasting, meditating, and listening. Don't let anything distract you from these practices.

According to Christ Jesus, giving time to distractions is a value judgment and a choice of what matters most. Be careful to redeem the time.

GOOD GOSSIP!

Luke 10:38-41 (NIV) As Jesus and his disciples were on their way, he came to a village where a woman named Martha opened her home to him. She had a sister called Mary who sat at the Lord's feet listening to what he said. But Martha was distracted by all the preparations that had to be made. She came to him and asked, "Lord don't you care that my sister has left me to do the work by myself? Tell her to help me!" "Martha, Martha," the Lord answered, "you are worried and upset about many things, but only one thing is needed. Mary has chosen what is better and it will not be taken away from her."

Ephesians 5:15-16 NIV

Be very careful, then, how you live—not as unwise but as wise, making the most of every opportunity, because the days are evil.

Ecclesiastes 9:10 NIV

Whatever your hand finds to do, do it with all your might, for in the realm of the dead, where you are going, there is neither working nor planning nor knowledge nor wisdom.

Let's Pray

Lord Jesus, our Father and our God, we thank You for Your precious gift of time. Your love for us is overflowing. Lord, help us to be mindful of our time here on this Earth, time you have given us. Time purposed for us to fulfill all that You have given us to do. Help us to remember that our days are numbered, and night is coming when no man nor woman can work from the grave. Whatever the assignments You give each of us, help us to value them and let our mindsets and actions say: "I must be about my Father's business." Father, help us to be wise and to stay alert. Help us to redeem the time. In the blessed name of Jesus, we pray.

Amen

Let us hold unswervingly to the hope we profess, for he who promised is faithful.

Hebrews 10:23 NIV

IFS, BUTS AND THENS

The hurt in her voice was unmistakable.

"If you loved me, I mean really, really loved me…"

He interrupted her sentence with a half-baked reply. "But I do."

"No, you don't. Because if you did then, you wouldn't treat me as you do."

Faking innocence he replied, "What are you talking about? What am I doing?"

"You're texting someone at three o'clock in the morning. I'm not asleep. I've been watching you the whole time. Don't make me go through your phone!"

Intensely, he responded. "Oh No! That's what you *don't* want to do! That spells trouble. When you go looking for trouble you are sure to find it!"

She shot back with, "Yes! And sometimes you don't have to go looking for it. Sometimes trouble finds you. I know something's up. For the last month you've been acting strange and there's talk going around about you continually being seen with some woman. So, who is she?"

IFS, BUTS AND THENS

He was busted and he knew it. He also knew that everybody in the streets knew what was going on except her and now the streets were talking. At this moment, he felt like a cornered rat with no way of escape. There was nothing left to do but come clean.

His voice dripped with insensitivity as he answered, "Listen! I've been meaning to talk to you. My path has crossed with someone else's. I have a lot of history with this person. They've come back into my life, and I want to see..., --no, I *need to see* where this goes."

She yelled, "That's it? *That's* what we're doing now! You're kicking me to the curb? We've made promises to each other! I've kept my promises, but you're breaking yours!"

"Hey, stuff happens," he replied. "I didn't plan this. Girl, I wanted to love you. But real talk, we've been together for almost a year, and I just don't think I can get there with you."

"Oh!" She replied. "And when did you realize this?" He ignored her question and said, "Sometimes things don't go like you planned or promised. The kind of love you give just doesn't match the kind I need. I realize that now. I invested much more in this relationship than you did."

Her voice cracked, "What do you mean by that?"

"I brought you all the way across country and paid for everything. I got this house we're living in. I did it all. And I'm not getting the kind of investment return that I'm looking for from you. Things have changed."

"Oh, now it's *my* fault? When it's you who's been creeping. Not me! But, if you think I'm going to let you pin the blame on me, then, you've got another thought coming. We're not playing that game!"

She continued on her rant, "I never should have left home but I was so ready to start out on this love journey with you. If only I hadn't packed in such a hurry. I packed my heart, with all of the promises you made to me, but in my haste and excitement, I forgot to pack my brain, too! I let you take me to the left when I should have stayed to the right. If I had done that, **then,** I wouldn't have ended up on this dead-end road with you!"

He countered, "But woman! You had no problem remembering to pack your constant complaining, insecurities, your suspicions, and your disrespect for my privacy. You *are* to blame. And you're right, it is a dead-end road. But now, Baby, I'm about to get up out of here. My path is leading me in another direction!"

Her voice cracked as she said, "Hear me when I say, You're no grand prize or anything to brag about either! As for me being a good 'investment return' for you here's an investment return you can take to the bank, and it's a promise too! You don't have to be the one to leave, because I'm leaving. And I don't think I ever really loved you, either!"

With a harsh laugh he responded, "Then, get to steppin! Your expiration date was yesterday!"

IFS, BUTS AND THENS

The Way I See It...

Ifs, buts, and *thens,* how many times have we used them pertaining to the decisions we make? My guess is that there are too many to number. I always say, "If-- *ifs* and *buts* were fruits and nuts *then,* this world would be an orchard. But in any orchard, you just can't plant peach and pecan seeds and expect a yield of apples and almonds."

Sometimes looking back on the *ifs, buts* and *thens* of our lives can bring about thoughts of regret and we find ourselves going down the "woulda- coulda- shoulda" rabbit holes.

Where we are in life today can be attributed to the decisions and promises we have made, received, and honored. It also applies to some of the decisions we have reversed and the promises we have not kept. It brings to mind the lyrics of an old *Frank Sinatra* hit titled, *That's Life.*

The lyrics seem to intimate someone just rolling along absorbing the bumps and bruises from the hits and misses of life and doing it all on their own.

There's living THAT life-- and then there's a way of living a *LIFE* that is fully sustained, abundantly empowered for good success, and promised by a faithful and loving God. However, He too, operates in *if's, but's,* and *then's,* according to His will. His *ifs, buts* and *thens* are keys that open the doors to the fullness and abundant fulfilment of

God's promises made manifest in our lives. How we respond to God's *ifs*, *buts*, and *thens*, is our choice.

The Bible has recorded well over 8,000 of God's promises. Many of them are conditional and are hinged to His *ifs*, *buts*, and *thens*. God's patterns and principles won't ever change, neither will His Word. And He keeps His promises.

IFS, BUTS AND THENS

GOOD GOSSIP!

Malachi 3:6 NIV

"I the Lord do not change."

Numbers 23:19 BSB

God is not a man, that He should lie, or a son of man, that He should change His mind. Does He speak and not act? Does He promise and not fulfill?

Genesis 4:7 NIV

"**If** you do what is right, will you not be accepted? **But** if you do not do what is right, sin is crouching at your door; it desires to have you, but you must rule over it."

Deuteronomy 11:22-23 NIV

If you carefully observe all these commands I am giving you to follow—to love the Lord your God, to walk in obedience to him and to hold fast to him— **then** the Lord will drive out all these nations before you, and you will dispossess nations larger and stronger than you.

2 Chronicles 7:14 NIV

If my people, who are called by my name, will humble themselves and pray and seek my face and turn from their wicked ways, **then** I will hear from heaven, and I will forgive their sin and heal their land.

John 15:5-7 NIV

I am the vine; you are the branches. **If** you remain in me and I in you, you will bear much fruit; apart from me you can do nothing. **If** you do not remain in me, you are like a branch that is thrown away and withers; such branches are picked up, thrown into the fire and burned. **If** you remain in me and my words remain in you, ask whatever you wish, and it will be done for you.

John 11:39-40 NIV

"But, Lord," said Martha, the sister of the dead man, "by this time there is a bad odor, for he has been there four days." Then Jesus said, "Did I not tell you that **if** you believe, you will see the glory of God?"

John 8:12 NIV

"I am the light of the world. Whoever follows me will never walk in darkness but will have the light of life."

Matthew 6:33 NIV

But seek first his kingdom and his righteousness, and all these things will be given to you as well.

John 4:13-14 NIV

Jesus answered, "Everyone who drinks this water will be thirsty again, but whoever drinks the water I give them will never thirst."

Hebrews 13:8 NIV

Jesus Christ is the same yesterday and today and forever.

Let's Pray

O loving and faithful Father, who watches over us, keeps us, and protects us, blessed be Your name. Father, we put our faith and trust in You, the One who will do just what He says. Fill our hearts and minds with the desire to please You through our obedience to Your will and way. By Your Holy Spirit help us to remember that You do not change, nor does Your Word. It is the same yesterday, today and forever. Help us to cherish our relationship with You through Christ our Savior and to do our part to meet the conditions of Your wonderful promises to us. For it is then and only then, that we have the right and the privilege to lay claims to Your promises and faithfully wait for You to fulfill each one of them according to Your will and in the fullness of Your timing.

In Jesus' name we pray. Amen

PART III
Spicy Information!

For I know the plans I have for you," declares the LORD, "plans to prosper you and not to harm you, plans to give you hope and a future.

Jeremiah 29:11 NIV

My Boaz is Married

The seasons of Spring and Summer had finally come into her life. Her heart had waited so long for them. But just as they had come without advance notice they abruptly left, or so it seemed.

As they withdrew, they tightly wrapped the love of her life in the permanence of death and carried him off with them. They did not ask her heart if it was in agreement with their unexpected departure. And to add insult to the hurt and pain of this young widow they carelessly left the door of her heart ajar for the entrance of a cold, dreary and uninvited companion. Its name was Winter.

Without warning it walked right into the chambers of her heart looking to take up perpetual residence. Not caring that its dark and somber presence was like a sponge soaking up all of the energy and space in her heart and blocking the light and warmth of day.

Just like the leaves of the trees in her backyard began to brown and brittle at the onset of a changing season, so did the leaves of her heart.

Hers was a fragile heart, now so damaged by this circumstance of life. It was unable to nourish itself because there was no sunlight, no comfort, so it sank deep down into the color of dusk.

Determined that her heart would never love again she sentenced it to eternal rest, and remembering a fairytale from her childhood, she changed its name to *Sleeping Beauty*. She prayed earnestly for her heart as it continued to sleep. However, closed eyes are not always the evidence of sleeping eyes and something was about to happen.

It was a phenomenon. In the midst of winter, spring appeared in the form of a man. She was drawn to his power and wisdom and to his gentleness. He was a force, the strong toughness of steel and yet the silky softness of velvet, and with these qualities he intentionally but gently pressed his way into the cold and lonely season of winter that had taken up squatter's rights in her life.

He had come to rescue her and had awakened and inspired in her a desire to rise again. He was the morning sun that climbed to the heights of the sky, shining its rays, piercing the dawn, as it greened the sleep-faded leaves of her dusk covered heart. She called him her Boaz. He overtook her with the ways of genuine kindness and generosity that love always desires to give. He was attentive, dependable, protective. She felt cared for and covered.

But even in all that he was to her, for them there would be no marital path to embark upon, because the one thing he could not be to her, was committed. He had already given his loyalty-consecrated love and commitment to another, given it to the one with whom he'd stood before God and made sacred vows. And most important to him was his commitment, love and loyalty to his Redeemer.

As the understanding of what had taken place, and of what would not take place, began to flood her heart and soul, she realized that this man she thought was her Boaz was really an instrument of God. He was an oasis; a season of God's redeeming love that had wedged itself inside of the wintery season that had occupied her heart with emptiness and despair.

And during this phenomenal season of redeeming love, she realized that all was not lost. Restoration had come in the hand of the Lord God Almighty and it was He who was her Redeemer and her Boaz through all seasons, and her heart could go on, her heart could love again...

The Way I See It...

Sometimes God ushers certain people into the lives of others at certain moments in time. They are there for specific reasons and sometimes only for a season.

These chosen vessels come alongside and pour out God's Gift of Love on those in need. They also carry with them the lessons God has specially designed to teach the intended individuals about life and themselves.

In God's hands these Godsends are His implements of redemption used to lift the desolate above the loneliness that they too often abide in behind the blinds-drawn windows and closed doors of their broken hearts.

It's a wonderful thing when restoration arrives. It's even more wonderful when the realization of God's ever-present redeeming love shines through as it did for the young widow in this story.

GOOD GOSSIP!

Psalm 71:20 NIV

"Though you have made me see troubles, many and bitter, you will restore my life again; from the depths of the earth you will again bring me up."

Isaiah 43:18-19 NIV

"Forget the former things;

do not dwell on the past.

See, I am doing a new thing!

Now it springs up; do you not perceive it?"

Isaiah 54:4-5 NIV

"…Remember no more the reproach of your widowhood. For your Maker is your husband — the Lord Almighty is his name — the Holy One of Israel is your Redeemer;

he is called the God of all the earth."

1st Peter 5:10 NIV

And the God of all grace, who called you to his eternal glory in Christ, after you have suffered a little while, will himself restore you and make you strong, firm and steadfast.

Let's Pray

O Blessed Savior, to You be Honor; Glory; Thanksgiving and Praise. There are seasons in our lives when You plant us; prune us; uproot us; and seasons when You, according to Your purpose, call us to suffer the agony of drinking from the cup of sorrow and despair. But through it all, Father, help us to remember that You are with us in ALL seasons. And that it is You, O God, who lifts our heads and heals our broken hearts. It is You who is our Redeemer. In Jesus' name, amen.

Cast your burden on the LORD, and he will sustain you; he will never permit the righteous to be moved.

Psalm 55:22

THE LUGGAGE UNDER HIS BED

It was hard to believe that five years had come and gone, and yet the memory of his time with her was as vivid and fresh in his mind as the breath of a newborn baby. He murmured her name, "Joy."

He remembered the softness of her voice and her sad eyes. He remembered word for word the conversation that would prove to be their last. But most of all he remembered the sudden emptiness he'd felt as he watched her walk out of his life. These memories stayed with him more than the sad memories of each of his two failed marriages. Somehow, he'd felt that this time things would be different. He would make this relationship work. At least that is what he'd planned. He was a sucker for playing the game of love, and he longed for his special someone. So, he'd taken a chance again, with Joy.

The newness of heart he felt with her was exhilarating but because he could not trust his newly changed heart or see the crystal ball future he needed to see, he reverted to the same actions of his past of infidelity, lying and selfishness. It was his wall of protection and self-preservation from the hurt he experienced with each failure. It was the weight of the two previously failed marriages that caused his feet to be wedged in his fear and stuck in the muddy idea of a possible third failure. And so, instead of playing to win in the game of love, he overcautiously played not to lose. In doing so, he perpetrated those actions upon this beautiful soul of a woman who had loved him in a way he had never known. And now she was gone, lost to him forever.

The smell of the hot buttered, rum and apple cider tea that he was drinking, brought his mind back to the present. As he took a sip, he sighed with the realization that of all the experiences of his adult life, losing Joy had crushed him the most and he could not let it go. It had become his second skin. It was his luggage. He carried it every day lugging it from here to there.

And each night in the confines of his tiny one room apartment he would put it down, so he could close his eyes to sleep. But not before he checked its contents piece by piece. He made sure that every thought and feeling of guilt, every reminder of the wrong and hurtful things he had done to the women in his life, and the wrong they'd done to him, including his mother, was still there intact and placed exactly how he wanted it.

Only then, would he lay his body down to sleep. And even in slumber, his luggage would always be close by, as he would neatly place it under the bed he slept on.

The Way I See It...

We all carry emotional luggage, often referred to as baggage. Some of us lug around more pieces than others. Our luggage **usually** contains the negative experiences from our childhood and past relationships that have not been settled.

In our own strength and understanding we use these negative experiences to build walls and fences of protection that serve to keep us from circling the same mountains over and over again. We hold on to these negative experiences **because** they help us manage our expectations of people, and keep at bay the sting of disappointment, pain, and rejection. We think we are operating in strength, but in reality, we are just allowing our emotional luggage (a.k.a. baggage), to sit on the thrones of our lives and rule.

Operating in our own strength is like trying to chew food with a mouth full of broken teeth. Nothing about our strength alone compares to the strength we have when we are in Jesus Christ. Because of the sacrifice He made for us and His gift of salvation we can unpack our history-filled luggage. **We can** let go of **what we lug around from place to place** filled with the things that occupy our minds, condemn us of sin, and saturate us with guilt. **Oh, but Hallelujah, and thanks be to God there is freedom in Christ.**

In Him we are free!

GOOD GOSSIP!

Matthew 11:28-30 ESV

"Come to me, all who labor and are heavy laden, and I will give you rest. Take my yoke upon you, and learn from me, for I am gentle and lowly in heart, and you will find rest for your souls. For my yoke is easy, and my burden is light."

Romans 8:1-2 ESV

There is therefore now no condemnation for those who are in Christ Jesus. For the law of the Spirit of life has set you free in Christ Jesus from the law of sin and death.

John 8:36 ESV

So if the Son sets you free, you will be free indeed.

Let's Pray

O, Merciful and Mighty God, help us to unyoke our minds, hearts, and spirits from our burdens we carry. Help us to place our burdens on the altar and leave them there. Father, we only want to be yoked to You, and Your way of living life. We seek Your guidance. Teach us, O Lord Jesus, that we may learn from You. We desire the rest that You offer us. In your Most High and Holy Name, we pray. Amen, and Amen.

For this reason, I am telling you, whatever things you ask for in prayer [in accordance with God's will], believe [with confident trust] that you have received them, and they will be given to you.

Mark 11:24 AB

Waiting

~~~~~~

Her crust filled eyelids unglued themselves as she was awakened by the rhythmic yet harsh sound of his snoring. She had always been the earlier riser of the two of them and his snoring had been her natural alarm clock for 20 years. He was a good man who'd never missed a night in her bed. And he had a license to be there because he was her husband.

She thanked her God for another day of life and the beginning of another day with her man. She thought about the events of the day before. She had been rummaging through a box of old papers that had been stored away in her office closet for more years than she'd been married. She had come across a frilly little pink handkerchief that partially covered a somewhat wrinkled envelope. In it was a somewhat tear-stained letter in her handwriting.

The vivid flashback of where she was and why she had written it was as clear as the diamonds that still sparkled on the now aged engagement ring and wedding band set she wore. She carefully opened the letter, recalling how she had put her faith and trust in God and embarked upon a journey that would take just that. A strong faith, a next level faith, a faith that waits on God. And as she delved into her memories of that time gone by, she began to read.

Saturday December 4, 1999, 7:50 A.M.

A letter to my unknown husband,

This is my first letter to you, it's something I've been contemplating doing for a while and now hopefully, by faith I write these letters to you.

You haven't made yourself known yet, but I know you are near. I feel your presence. A feeling and a knowing so strong. I have begun to thank my Father for you already. I thank Him that He has designed you just for me, and me just for you.

I thank Him for the great sense of humor he has given you and for your sensitivity to my needs. The way you listen to what I have to say, the way you are so affectionate towards me, the way you treat me as a blessing more precious than gold.

I thank Him that He has given you a humble spirit, wise and kind and forgiving. I thank Him that He has made you pleasing to my eyes, not just to the eyes of my physical sight, but to the eyes of my heart and my understanding.

I Thank Him that you are a Godly man and the covering you provide for me is an anointed one. I thank Him that you are submissive to His leading and direction and that you hear His voice and want to obey. I thank Him that you are rich in relationship with Him and His Word, and your life bears the fruit of this.

I thank Him for giving me to a man I can respect, a man whom my spirit is so willing to submit to. A man who will be the priest of our home, who will wash me in the water of the Word. I thank Him for your understanding of the importance of and power of praying together, of communicating with each other. I thank Him that you are able to teach me in an understanding and peaceful way. That we are able to agree to disagree without harboring animosity but always ready for an opportunity or experience that can teach us both and bring accord and agreement.

I have been waiting for you for some time now, delighting myself in my Father, our Father. He has heard my prayer and is answering as I write. For He said to me, a few days ago, "I am doing a new thing. Now it springs up, do you not perceive it?" I thank and praise Him by the measure of faith He has placed in me.

Well, I'm getting up now. I have lots of things to do. Buy groceries, hang Christmas lights, and cover some shelves in the kitchen.

Be sweet my love, talk to you again soon...

Your Lady in Waiting

When she had finished reading her letter she folded it making sure the freshly formed wetness in the corners of her eyes could not add new tear stains. She carefully returned it to its envelope. She would show it to her husband today as a confirmation and a reminder that God hears and He always answers whether it be yes, no, or wait. She had prayerfully, thankfully, and faithfully waited on the Lord and He had answered. In the Spring of 2004, she became a Mrs. when she married the man of her prayers and dreams. As she was leaving her cluttered office closet she chuckled to herself and said, "Lord, the only thing I forgot to ask of You was that he NOT be a snoring man."

The Way I See It...

Ya gotta have faith! Ya gotta believe! But have faith in what? Believe in what? Are you believing in the words of the "name it and claim it" gospel, or are you believing in the Word of God? Are you putting your faith in the situation you are praying for or are you putting it solely in God? Be sure that your faith is in Him alone. It will be your greatest act of doing what is good, and what is right. Then, patiently stand back and wait for the answer. Watch how the Lord responds to your very specific asks and prayers that of course, must be in accordance with his ways, thoughts, and will for your life. Will it be a yes, no, or wait? That, I cannot say, but what I will say is: "Wait, I say. Wait on the Lord!"

GOOD GOSSIP!

Hebrews 11:1 NKJ

Now faith is the substance of things hoped for, the evidence of things not seen.

James 1:6 NLT

But when you ask him, be sure that your faith is in God alone.

Galatians 6:9 NLT

So let's not get tired of doing what is good. At just the right time we will reap a harvest of blessing if we don't give up.

Psalm 27:14 NLT

Wait patiently for the LORD. Be brave and courageous. Yes, wait patiently for the LORD.

Let's Pray

O Omnipotent Father God! You who are also Omniscient and Omnipresent. We praise You and thank You for Your presence in our lives. Thank You for the measure of faith you have given each of us. Lord, may our measure of faith be deeply rooted and continually developed as we journey onward and upward on the King's Highway towards Heaven. In Jesus' name. Amen.

… for the battle is not yours, but God's.

2 Chronicles 20:15 KJV.

Clutched Pearls

~~~~~~~~~~~~~~~~~~~~~~~

"Every time I turn around you are headed to that church! All day service Sunday, Bible study Wednesday, Prayer meeting Friday. What, you sleeping with the deacons now? You gonna stop this nonsense! Because I'm gonna put an end to this!"

She did not answer him. Instead, she whispered, "Lord, please! Strengthen me."

And she quickly left the house, slamming the door on his words as he yelled, "RAMONA! I said you ain't goin' nowhere!"

Now she had returned to what she had started calling the house of woe.

She remembered his attitude towards her and the nasty words he'd spat out at her as she was leaving for evening prayer service at the church. That's how he was when he was in a gin and tonic frame of mind. Her hope was that by now he'd left the house and if he hadn't, she decided she would just ignore him.

She inserted her key into the lock on the front door and as she opened it the first thing she spotted was her brand-new study Bible alongside the Bible she had bought for him months ago. Both Bibles were laid open with their pages torn out, ripped in pieces, and scattered across the living room floor.

Even through all the mean words he was constantly pelting her with about her involvement with the church, she had tried so many times to talk to him about his lifestyle and the things of God. It had been exactly one year and six months since she'd accepted the gift of salvation and had hit the ground running in her zest for learning and serving the Lord, and growing in His grace. But her husband had remained stagnant. He continued to embrace the darkness of his worldliness with no evidence of a desire to move to the Light. She and he were no longer "birds of the same feather." Nevertheless, she had vowed to keep praying for her man. She still loved him. But this Bible-destroying incident was so much more than she was prepared for.

Her old ways of physically handling issues that hurt and enraged her rose up in her spirit. She'd always been a fighter, adept at defending herself. And her husband bore the permanent bite marks in his chest that proved it. She felt the soft cover that had shrouded her heart since coming to Jesus instantly morph into a slab of cold hard concrete, and she knew there was about to be a brawl.

"RAYMOND DIGGS!" She screamed, as she made her way past the shredded Bibles and into the bedroom. There he was knocked out, sprawled sideways across the bed with an empty gin bottle lying beside him.

The sight of him in that condition drained her of her rage. Now deflated, wearily, she turned around, left the bedroom and walked back into the living room. By now her tears were flowing. She knew what she'd read in the first letter to the Corinthians where the Apostle Paul spoke about living in a house with an unsaved husband. She shook her head in the movement that means, "No," because she also knew that for his safety, and her spiritual health and sanity, they would have to separate. She cried out.

"Lord, I just can't do this anymore. You see what's happening. You know I've tried. Please tell me what to do, please show me what to do. No one knows but you what I'm going through in this house. Help me, Lord, rescue me! Show me what to do!"

She plopped down onto one of the livingroom chairs and as she partially landed on the chair's armrest she felt and heard the crackle of paper. One of the pages from the mutilated Bibles had landed there. Wiping her tears, she picked it up. The hairs on the back of her neck began to stand up as she read what was left of it, *"The battle is not yours, but God's."*

She felt the piercing power of those words as they infiltrated her heart. The Holy Spirit had entered the room. The Lord had swiftly answered, and she knew that she must stay. She held God's words on the tattered page to her chest clutching them as if they were precious pearls. And to her…they were.

The Way I See It...

"How can two walk together unless they be agreed?"

Amos 3:3 KJV

Agreement is the place of power. Unity and oneness are a must for there to be success in any partnership.

A partnership can consist of more than just two people. And it is true that there is strength in numbers. But it is also true that there is the possibility of partners having different points of view on things.

Jesus said:

"Where two or three are gathered in my name there I am in the midst of them."

Matthew 18:20 KJV

If you have come into a partnership and you become the only one there who has gathered in Jesus' name, make sure your agreement is with Him. Follow God's Word. It's the only thing He places above His name. No matter how large or small the size of a partnership, the oneness needed for success is only a sure thing when you partner in unity with the Lord.

GOOD GOSSIP!

Psalm 46:10 KJV

Be still, and know that I am God. I will be exalted among the heathen, I will be exalted in the earth.

Proverbs 3:5-6 KJV

Trust in the LORD with all thine heart; and lean not unto thine own understanding. In all thy ways acknowledge him, and he shall direct thy paths.

Psalm 138:2-3 KJV

I will worship toward thy holy temple, and praise thy name for thy lovingkindness and for thy truth: for thou hast magnified thy word above all thy name. In the day when I cried thou answeredst me, *and* strengthenedst me *with* strength in my soul.

Let's Pray

O Victorious Father God, please lead and guide us in the way of your righteousness. Saturate us with Your peace and strength when we are surrounded by turmoil and unrest. When the enemy swoops in to destroy us help us to stand on Your Word. Let the Fruit of Your Spirit operate in us and through us as You go before us in battle and defend us from behind. Help us to remember that our fearfully and wonderfully made bodies were bought and paid for with the precious blood of Jesus. Father, fill us with the desire to glorify You, and the wherewithal to go where You want us to go, to say what You want us to say.

Help us to do what You want us to do in obedience to You. We ask this in the great name of Jesus Christ our Lord, and Savior. Amen.

PART IV
Can't Keep This to Myself

By this my Father is glorified, that you bear much fruit and so prove to be my disciples.

John 15:8 ESV

Touch it, Feel it, Taste it

Rosa: Where am I going to find fruit good enough for the Executives' meeting? I wish they'd asked someone else to get this stuff. I don't know nothin' bout' pickin' no fruit!

Dee: Ha! You sound like that *Gone With the Wind* actress, Butterfly McQueen.

Rosa: You're showing your age, girl!

Dee: Why don't you try the Whole Fruits Market over on Chester?

Rosa: You mean *Whole Foods*, don't you?

Dee: No, I mean Whole Fruit. I was always told to check for the color and the smell. But I'll go with you because if you come back here with something that ain't right they gon' be in the breakroom talkin' bout you all week.

Rosa: Thanks Dee, I know that's right! You know I'm new to this team. We Brown Girls have to work smarter, and I need all the 'Brownie' points I can get!

Dee. That Brown Girl joke is so corny. But no problem, let's go check out some fruit.

TOUCH IT, FEEL IT, TASTE IT

The Way I See It...

I overheard someone say: "If you gently squeeze any fruit in question and it feels as soft as your cheek, it's past its prime. If it feels as solid as your forehead, it's not ripe. If it feels like the end of your nose where the cartilage is, it's ripe. Buy it and eat it."

Personally speaking, I think the best way to tell is to taste it; sample it. Most merchants don't allow us to inspect the fruit we buy in that way.

Ahh, but there is another kind of Fruit that CAN be sampled. It is the Fruit of the Spirit: Love, Joy, Peace, Patience, Kindness, Goodness, Faithfulness, Gentleness and Self-control. You can judge for yourself who is or isn't operating in them.

Okay...okay, I know the Bible says we should judge not, lest we be judged! And I'm good with that. But we CAN be FRUIT inspectors! We'll know they are HIS disciples by their love. Have you inspected someone's Fruit today? Have you inspected your own Fruit today?

GOOD GOSSIP!

Matthew 7:16 KJV
"Ye shall know them by their fruits."

Let's Pray

O Lord, as we walk, please light our paths with eyes that see, ears that hear, and hearts that discern. Let the Fruit of Your Spirit bloom and ripen in us yielding Love, Joy, Peace, Patience, Kindness, Goodness, Faithfulness, Gentleness and Self-Control. In Jesus' name. Amen!

Do nothing out of selfish ambition or vain conceit. Rather, in humility value others above yourselves,

Philippians 2:3

SENT ONE...WENT ONE

Carla walks into the ladies' room to find Florence in tears.

Carla: Why are you crying? What's wrong?

Florence: Everything's wrong. I'm in over my head with this project. Everyone's talking about me and not in a nice way.

Carla: If I may ask, how did you end up doing the annual project? Don't you usually do the quarterly report…? You're great at that Plus, you know Gina always does the annual project.

Florence: Oh, so now you're in Gina's court? You're supposed to be MY friend.

Carla: No, I'm not in Gina's court and yes, I am YOUR friend. But I'm always going to keep it real with you.

Florence: Gina's not the only one around here who can do things that require a high degree of brain power. I'm just as intelligent as she is, even more because, I have a degree! She doesn't!

Carla: Everyone knows you have a degree. You never stop telling us about it. People think you're full of yourself.

Florence: Is that what's being said? Who's saying that? Well, it doesn't change the fact that I have one.

Carla: Girlfriend, a degree? That just means you have a portion of knowledge about something. Remember, all you might know is not all there is to know.

Florence: What does that even mean?

Carla: Did you ever stop to think that maybe God chose Gina for that particular assignment, and "sent" her to that department for a specific reason? Did you even pray about it? Probably not. You just took your degree…and matters, into your own hands and "went". Now you're stuck. Florence, sometimes it's not what you know, it's "Who" you know…

The Way I See It...

No matter how bad you want to, you just can't do everything someone else has been specifically chosen and equipped to do. When you try to be something you're not, it doesn't fare well for you. God doesn't call us to something only to leave us to fend for ourselves. Read about the lives of Moses, Esther, and Gideon (just to name a few). God equips those He chooses to send.

Are you a "Sent One" or a "Went One"?

GOOD GOSSIP!

Proverbs 3:5-6 NLT

Trust in the LORD with all your heart; do not depend on your own understanding.

Seek his will in all you do, and he will show you which path to take.

Galatians 5:25-26 NLT

Since we are living by the Spirit, let us follow the Spirit's leading in every part of our lives. Let us not become conceited, or provoke one another, or be jealous of one another.

Hebrews 13:21 NLT

May he equip you with all you need for doing his will. May he produce in you, through the power of Jesus Christ, every good thing that is pleasing to him.

All glory to him forever and ever! Amen.

Philippians 2:13 NLT

For God is working in you, giving you the desire and the power to do what pleases **him**.

Let's Pray

Lord Jesus, help us to stay on the path that you have chosen for us. You have set us all on one path with many lanes. That one path is to serve you; to do what it is you have called us to do. As your children, it is so easy for us to look to the right and to the left and want what we see someone else doing. Help us to inquire of you and trust you enough as you direct our paths. Lord, help us to stay in our lanes. We ask this in your faithful and precious name. Amen.

You received God's Spirit when he adopted you as his own children. Now we call him, "Abba, Father."

Romans 8:15 NLT

Family Perks

The exciting information she had just received was so hot it scorched and blistered her lips and tongue. It had to be told. She hit the call button on her phone and impatiently waited for the Hello from the other end. She knew the cooling relief of satisfaction would only come once she was able to pour her news into the ear of her "play" cousin on the other end.

"Hello?"

"I cannot believe it! No way! Are you serious?"

The voice on the other end responded. "You can't believe what? Am I serious about what? What's going on with you? Calm down. Stop yelling! And talk so I can understand you."

"Girrrl, I won first prize in the GGM sweepstakes!"

"You're lying! Stop playing!"

"I'm serious, listen to all that I won! Round trip 1st class plane tickets to France, premier hotel accommodations, free meals, free chauffeur service and VIP passes at the Yolanda Adams and Kirk Franklin concert."

"I know you're taking me with you seeing as I'm your BFF. Right? That's right in time for my birthday. When do we leave?"

FAMILY PERKS

There was a pause. "Well…uhh, no."

"But I'm your best friend."

The disappointment in her BFF's voice was unmistakable.

"I'm not going to be your plus one. I don't believe this! Why?"

"My Auntie is my plus one. There's no way I can pass over her; no way she's not going to get to enjoy this. And just keeping it real, although you and I are good friends it just wouldn't be right to take you and not her. After all, she's my family. And you know how much family matters to me."

"Yeah, I know that. Your auntie has always been like a mother to me…I get it. I should've entered that sweepstakes too. Maybe I would've won, and I would've taken you".

The contest winner replied, "Are you trying to make me feel bad?"

"No, no, we're still cool because I'm going anyway! I have enough money saved to take this trip to France. I won't get the royal treatment you guys will get and all the other perks that come with flying first class. We won't be sitting together on the plane, and I won't have a banging hotel suite like you will, but that's okay. Hotel rooms are only for sleeping anyway."

Hearing her BFF's voice perk up she replied, "I think I dodged a bullet."

"Why do you think that?"

"Because even though we always tell people we are blood, if we really were, it would have been very hard for me to choose between my auntie and her daughter."

The Way I See It...

There's Grace and There's GRACE!

Everyone gets to experience the warmth of the sun and the coolness of the rain whether they're just or unjust, righteous or unrighteous.

That's God providing His common grace.

But...

♪ ♪ "God sent His Son, they called Him Jesus. He came to love, heal and forgive. He lived and died to buy my pardon. An empty grave is there to prove my savior lives." ♪

- G&B Gaither

That's God providing His SPECIAL GRACE, His SAVING GRACE for His family. And that kind of grace comes through faith and believing in Jesus Christ.

GOOD GOSSIP!

Ephesians 2:19-20 NLT

So now you Gentiles are no longer strangers and foreigners. You are citizens along with all of God's holy people. You are members of God's family. Together, we are his house, built on the foundation of the apostles and the prophets. And the cornerstone is Christ Jesus himself.

John 1:12-13 BSB

But to all who did receive Him, to those who believed in His name, He gave the right to become children of God— children born not of blood, nor of the desire or will of man, but born of God.

Let's Pray

O Abba Father! Our God and our King! We thank You for Your unmerited favor and the blessings we receive as your children. We thank You that You have adopted us into Your family and made us a part of Your household. We are rich to overflowing with Your love, Your grace and Your mercy. Thank You that there is no GOOD thing You will withhold from us. Give us a willingness to share with others these truths we have come to know through our personal experiences of being Your children. And share that it is only through Christ that we become children of God. Some may not know or realize that while we are all Your creatures created by You, we are not all Your children. Use us as your instruments to touch hearts and open eyes so they too can experience the love-filled benefits of being a part of Your family and the great blessing of being able to say:

"My FATHER is the KING."

In Jesus' name. Amen.

For God has said, "I will never fail you. I will never abandon you."

Hebrews 13:5 NLT

The Terrible T's

※─◆─※

She'd been knocked to the canvas with blows to her head and one-two punches to her soft underbelly, where her spirit lived. The hard knocks of life and the current pile up of new problems with their old entanglements and temptations just seemed to hang on. So did the never ending chatter about her, and how she was living her life.

At first she heard the referee giving the count: one…two… three, she was fading in and out of consciousness…*What's happening to me?*

In her head she recognized the sound of her silent voice, her desperate thoughts. *"Lord I've tried…I've cried…I've prayed…but I'm just not able to let it go. Why do I allow myself to say yes when I know I should be saying no? It only brings me more pain, more trials, more mistreatment…more problems. I can't fight anymore. What's the use of trying? Even when I shake my fist at you, you don't answer…You're nowhere to be found…where are you…where are you when I need you?"*

And then, from what seemed far away she began to hear the count again: six, seven… the voice of who she thought was the referee got louder, and clearer. She felt the warmth of his breath. His face was as close to hers as the number eight is to the number nine. She heard him whisper:

"I'm here, I've always been here. Look for me in the Word I've left for you. You've looked everywhere but there. My Word is your way out. It's your way of escape. That is your way to victory. Trust my promises. Let go of what was. And pray in the Spirit, my child. Pray in the Spirit."

And so, she did...

The Way I See It...

Sometimes when traumatic situations happen in life one might feel alone, feel no one else has ever had to contend with an ordeal such as theirs.

Don't think for a moment that times of Testing and Temptation will not come. It can be unnerving and yet awe-inspiring at the same time. It will put your faith, patience, and diligence in reading God's Word on trial as to your loyalty and obedience to God.

This is where we get to see who and where we really are in our walk of faith, something God, our Father already knows.

These times are for our testing and refining. And for those who endure as they travail through the valleys of temptation, trials and testing, they shall come out with a faith that is strong, solid, and more precious and greater than the purest silver and gold.

GOOD GOSSIP!

1 Corinthians 10:13 MSG
No test or temptation that comes your way is beyond the course of what others have had to face. All you need to remember is that God will never let you down; he'll never let you be pushed past your limit; he'll always be there to help you come through it.

1 Peter 4:12-13 MSG
Friends, when life gets really difficult, don't jump to the conclusion that God isn't on the job. Instead, be glad that you are in the very thick of what Christ experienced. This is a spiritual refining process, with glory just around the corner.

Psalms 66:10-12 MSG
He trained us first, passed us like silver through refining fires, Brought us into hardscrabble country, pushed us to our very limit. Road tested us inside and out, took us to hell and back; Finally he brought us to this well-watered place.

Let's Pray

You, Father God, are our strength. You uphold us with Your righteous hand and keep our feet from slipping. Refine us to be used for Your glory. It is only by Your power, and through You that we walk in victory. Thank You for Your love, Your Holy Spirit, and our Savior Jesus Christ, one God eternal, present in our lives. In Jesus' name. Amen.

PART V
Rumor Has It!

For as he thinketh in his heart, so is he

Proverbs 23:7 KJV

Junk Food

~~~~~~~~~~~~~

She was going home.

Her scheduled Uber service to the airport was to pick her up in four hours. Her mind was still preoccupied. Lingering, piercing and painful feelings of rejection pummeled her heart. It was making her hungry. She needed to eat. She just wanted something to **erase the hurt,** at least for a little while.

Moments later, she walked into her favorite fast-food eatery.

"I'll have a double cheeseburger, fries, and a cookies and cream float, please."

As she waited for her order to be filled, she glanced through the glass window of the storefront. She happened to notice an overly large-figured woman standing on the outside, looking through the store window and staring intently at her.

"Who is THAT?" She murmured.

Her thought was quickly interrupted as she heard the counter person call out her order number. As she stepped forward, to pick it up, the woman outside of the store stepped forward too. In that instant she realized that the overly large-figured woman staring at her was her own reflection. She didn't even recognize herself anymore.

A year ago, she'd decided to apply to the highest-ranking school on the West coast for her acting career. She'd saved her money, and the following year she left the country roads of her southern hometown and made her way to California. Once there she'd applied for admission to the *Cal Arts School of Theatre, Film and Television*, submitting all the documents required. A month later she received their response.

She remembered how her trembling fingers felt like unbendable sticks while opening the envelope. She remembered the audible gasp that escaped her lips as she read the opening sentence. "We regret to inform you…" She remembered stopping right there and tossing the letter across her room. It was one week before she picked it up again and read its entirety.

After further contact with the school, she learned that while she had met the SAT and GPA scores by the skin of her teeth, it was the scores from her required audition and portfolio submission that were not good enough. During those next few weeks, she seeded her mind with discouraging thoughts and words about herself. In her despair she saw herself as hopeless, useless and defeated. Her only comfort was her junk food, and she medicated herself with it religiously. Now, three months to the day that she'd opened that letter, here she was, headed back home to country living.

Much later, while up in the air, she spent the six-hour plane ride thinking about how she would break the news she'd kept hidden from her faithful, but critical mother for the past six months. She opened the bag of "goodies" she had brought along to keep her company. Cookies…, candy…, chips…, Ding

Dongs…, and soft drinks. As she filled her stomach with each piece of the junk food, her mind, too, nibbled away at her self-esteem. Chips…*I should have known better than to try.* Cookies… *I'm just not good enough.* Candy…*I can't do anything right.* Ding Dongs…*Nothing ever works out for me.* Soft drinks…*I'm so stupid.*

Once the plane landed, her mother was there to meet her.

"Hi, Mom. I made it in one piece. Can't wait to get to the house."

Her mother hugged and kissed her, and responded, "What have you been eating for the last six months? Or should I ask, what's been eating you? You need to go on a diet!"

JUNK FOOD

The Way I See It...

"Sow a thought and you reap an action. Sow an act and you reap a Habit. Sow a habit and you reap a character. Sow a character and you reap a destiny." -Ralph Waldo Emerson

I think what Emerson was saying was: your spoken thoughts are the words you utter, and your words give birth to your world. Be careful what you think, be careful what you say. Because your mind is always listening, waiting, and ready to support your thoughts which become your actions.

The Bible says:

Death and life are in the power of the tongue… (Proverbs 18:21 KJV).

A Pastor's remarks provoked me to thought when he said: "There are only a few things in life that we have no control over."

I began to think about some of them. There's death, the past, natural disasters, and the weather. But what we can control are our thoughts, words and actions. Here's an example. I'm a foodie. I love to eat. So, I tend to think of it in terms of diet. In this God-made creation that I call Me, I have my soul, my spirit, and my flesh. All of them have to be fed. Well, every now and then, a frosted donut with my coffee tastes good to my flesh. But convincing myself that I can have two of those delicious, frosted donuts with my coffee, every morning without fail is neglecting the other parts of this God-made creation that I call Me. It's empty calories.

When we leave this Earth, whether we're going to one of those many mansions Jesus talks about, or if we're going somewhere else, the flesh isn't coming with us. It can't go where we're going. Only our souls and our spirits will make that trip. And that's a fact.

Therefore, let's take diligent care of our spirits and our souls. Both will respond to the nutritious and nourishing truth of God's Word. Feeding on His Truth will keep us healthy.

Let us saturate our thoughts and words with who God says we are, and how He sees us. Keep feeding on His goodness and trustworthiness and how much He loves us. Protect the mind and guard the heart. Then when trouble comes calling (and it will), your mind, heart, soul, and spirit will support and follow God's truth.

GOOD GOSSIP!

Romans 12:2 ESV

Do not be conformed to this world, but be transformed by the renewal of your mind, that by testing you may discern what is the will of God, what is good and acceptable and perfect.

Psalm 107:9 ESV

For he satisfies the longing soul, and the hungry soul he fills with good things.

Romans 7:18 ESV

For I know that nothing good dwells in me, that is, in my flesh.

Proverbs 4:23 NLT

Guard your heart above all else, for it determines the course of your life.

Philippians 4:8 NLT

And now, dear brothers and sisters, one final thing. Fix your thoughts on what is true, and honorable, and right, and pure, and lovely, and admirable. Think about things that are excellent and worthy of praise.

Let's Pray

O Loving and Faithful Father God, who is like You? There is no one. For You alone are worthy and You alone are great. Help us to lean and depend on Your Word. Help us to keep at the forefront of our minds that You love us more than we could ever imagine. Help us to see ourselves as You see us, fearfully and wonderfully made. Help us to cast down and bring into captivity every thought, every word and action that would exalt itself against You. By Your power help us to fast from, and even starve our flesh. Help us to remember it all begins with a word. In the beginning was the Word. Help us to nourish and encourage our souls, our spirits, our hearts and our minds by feeding and feasting on Your love, and Your Word. Lord, feed us till we want no more. For You, Lord Jesus, are our Bread of Heaven. In Your Precious Name we pray. Amen.

I was glad when they said to me, "Let us go into the house of the LORD."

Psalms 122:1 NKJV

PRICELESS {ACT TWO}

———⚜———

The woman took notice of the way the straight grain of the mahogany wood was visible even though it was thickly coated with what looked like a rich hue of dark maple syrup.

As she sat there her fingers glided over a portion of the smooth, polished surface it offered. She was impressed with its image. It looked somewhat regal and archaic. She leaned against its sturdy, fixed back for support. She felt its strength, and it gave her a sense of stability and calm. Its dark, polished surface caught her reflection. It saddened her. She did not like the person that was staring back at her.

Yet, there was an appealing softness she felt as its fleece-like cushion welcomed her near middle-aged body. She would never forget this day, nor the feelings she experienced while sitting in this majestic pew. Because on this day, she heard God's voice say:

"Come. Sit with Me, I am the Ancient of Days. I will hold you and support you. I will give you strength. I will do a new thing in you and give you a new look."

She stood up, stepped out into the aisle, walked up to the altar, and accepted God's priceless gift of salvation.

PRICELESS {ACT TWO}

The Way I See It...

Traveling down life's highways forgetting who you are, or never knowing who you are, can place you in a world of trouble. Being disconnected or untethered you will be like a feather, sometimes easily and gently wafting through the air, sometimes harshly pushed by a strong blast of wind and all the while drifting downward into the inevitability of unlikeness and anonymity.

It can be a very lonely existence. But when you don't know who you are, you just don't know. You don't know that you were made in the image of God. You don't know that you were created for His good pleasure. You don't know that you were created with a purpose. You don't know that your identity is in Jesus Christ.

When our Father and our God looks at us He doesn't see us as we might see ourselves. He sees us through His gift of grace, mercy and salvation that is freely given to us through the Blood of Jesus. And how does our Lord Jesus see us? What does He say about you? How does He define you? The answer to those questions is found in His Word. Read it. Get to know Jesus. You will find that you are not an orphan without an identity. You belong to the family of God.

GOOD GOSSIP!

Genesis 1:27 NLT

So God created human beings in his own image. In the image of God he created them; male and female he created them.

Colossians 1:16-17

Everything was created through him and for him.

Psalm 139:14 NKJV

I will praise You for I am fearfully and wonderfully made;

Romans 8:29

For God knew his people in advance, and he chose them to become like his Son, so that his Son would be the firstborn[2] among many brothers and sisters.

Acts 17:28-29

For in him we live and move and exist. As some of your own poets have said, 'We are his offspring.'

Ephesians 2:10 NLT

For we are God's masterpiece. He has created us anew in Christ Jesus, so we can do the good things he planned for us long ago.

---

[2] https://biblehub.com/nlt/romans/8.htm

Let's Pray

Most Holy Father and Lord, help us to understand what it means to be made in Your image. Help us to see ourselves as You see us. That we may live in our true identity. Because of Your sacrifice we are new creatures. Help us to realize that in You, Lord, we walk in pureness. We are Your blameless and forgiven children. Help us to meditate on how much we mean to You. You are our loving Father, and our Father is the KING. In Jesus' name. Amen

EPILOGUE

And God said…

In the first Book of the Bible, Genesis Chapter One, God spoke to His creation. He communicated. And He said quite a lot. From all that God said, came His creation of life in all its various forms and fleshes.

Communication is the basis of life.

If our organs and body systems did not, or could not, communicate with our brain, we would die.

We communicate through our verbal and body language. The major functions of communicating are to inform, to persuade and to motivate. Gossip is a form of communication. Yes, it's looked down on, and not worthy of respect. There's no denying that. But gossip still checks all three of the boxes of the functions of communication. Informing, persuading, and motivating are tools for forming human bonding, and sometimes even trust. Gossip can transcend its negative meaning and build bridges of social and Godly connections when it informs, motivates, encourages, evokes and invokes the goodness of the Lord through the sharing of His Holy Word.

EPILOGUE

"I heard He dries weeping eyes.

I heard He can do the impossible.

Oh, get to know Jesus.

I heard He heals the sick." -Javonta Patton

Now THAT'S some GOOD GOSSIP!

ACKNOWLEDGEMENTS

Pamela A. Francis, my Editor Extraordinaire and #1 sounding board whose calm disposition and endurance is only exceeded by her editorial expertise.

The late John McNees, my very patient Illustrator/Cover and Book Designer who worked closely with me on several books and passed away before the completion of this project. John had the amazing gift of being able to flesh out the imagery in my head. May he rest in peace.

Pastor Henry P. Davis III, who thought it not robbery of his time to read and critique several excerpts from this book. Pastor Davis always gave me his candid view.

Adam Powell (a.k.a. Major Maestro), recording artist, filmmaker, modern farmer and landscaper who took valuable time during his landscaping visits to sit on my front porch and chat with me about writing habits and goals. Unbeknownst to him those talks motivated me to push past a season of writer's block.

My Pastor, Daemon S. Moss whose preached sermon of Sunday January 7, 2024, titled "*Everything Begins With a Word*" was the inspiration for "Junk Food" one of the last stories of my book.

Rae'L Jackson-Smith, Owner of Rae J. Photography, is a wonderful photographer with a real eye for the camera. Her contagious excitement, encouragement and gracious gift of an author photo session was a blessing.

ACKNOWLEDGEMENTS

A special thanks to Mohamed Maghchich. I was desperately in need of someone to assume the mantle left behind after the sudden death of my longtime book designer. I began my search and pored over the profiles of at least thirty book designers, formatters, and typesetters. However, it was Mohamed Maghchich's profile, as well as the great reviews he has received, that stood out to me. He has been a Godsend. Mohamed's professionalism, kindness and patience has been paramount in helping me get to the finish line.

MEET THE AUTHOR

~ Shirley Francis-Salley ~

Entering the world of adult fiction, Shirley Francis-Salley, a children's ministry teacher and award-winning author, guides her audience down new pathways in Christ. For more than ten years she has been dedicated to a mission of creating Sunday school lessons that make the word of God appealing and practical in the daily lives of kids of all ages. She has published children's books, articles, short stories, skits, Bible dramas, song lyrics, board games, Sunday school lessons and lesson plans. Shirley's other published books include *Shifty Characters, Fruit Scoop, and Tweens and Teens Praising the Lord from Alpha to Omega – and Everything in Between, Busy Body, God loves animals from A to Z - But Not as Much as He Loves Me.*

As the matriarch of a large and extended family, she has countless opportunities to talk about the situations of everyday life that confront us no matter what age we are. Shirley resides in Chester County, South Carolina.